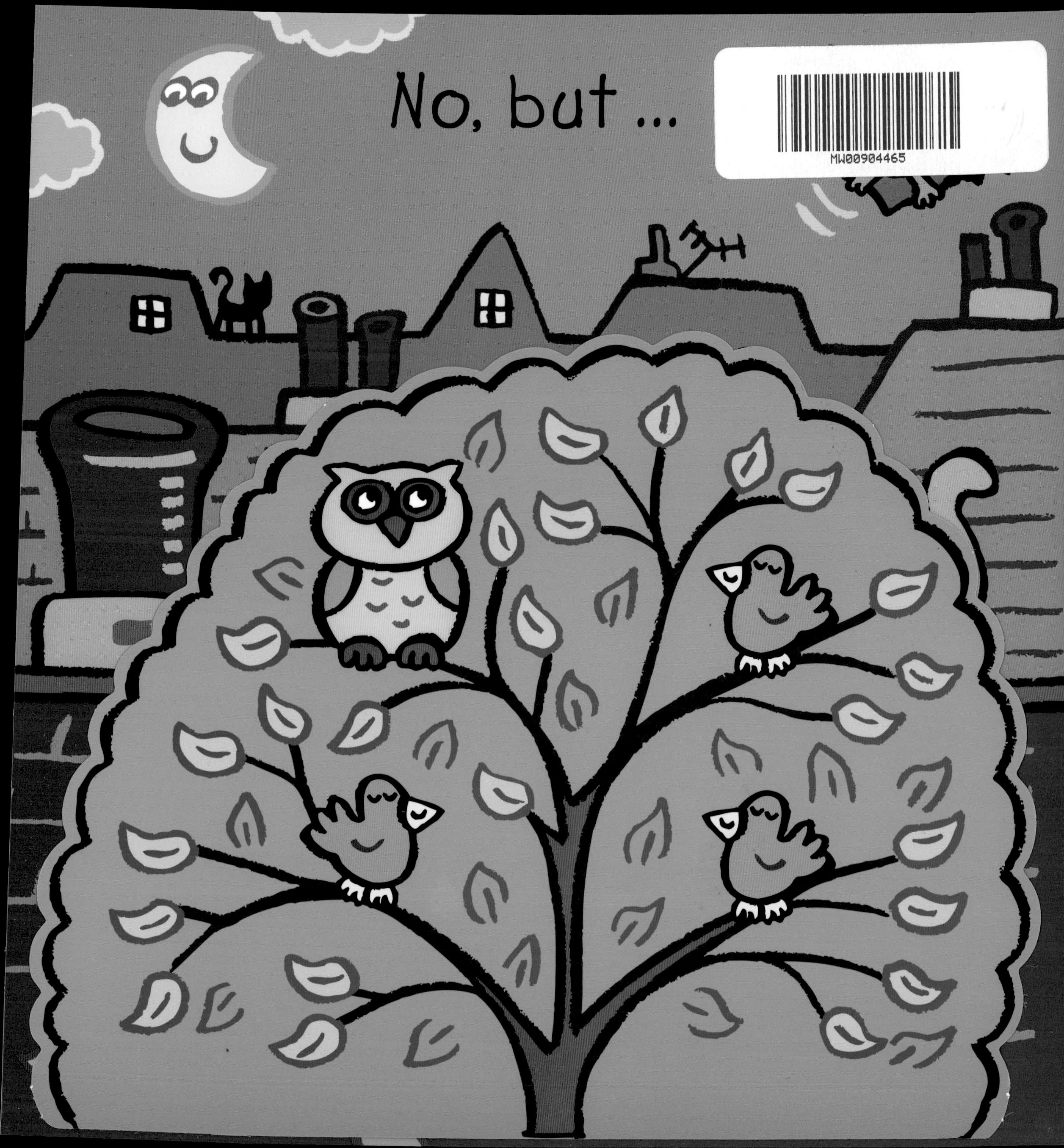
No, but ...

Do ducks dig?

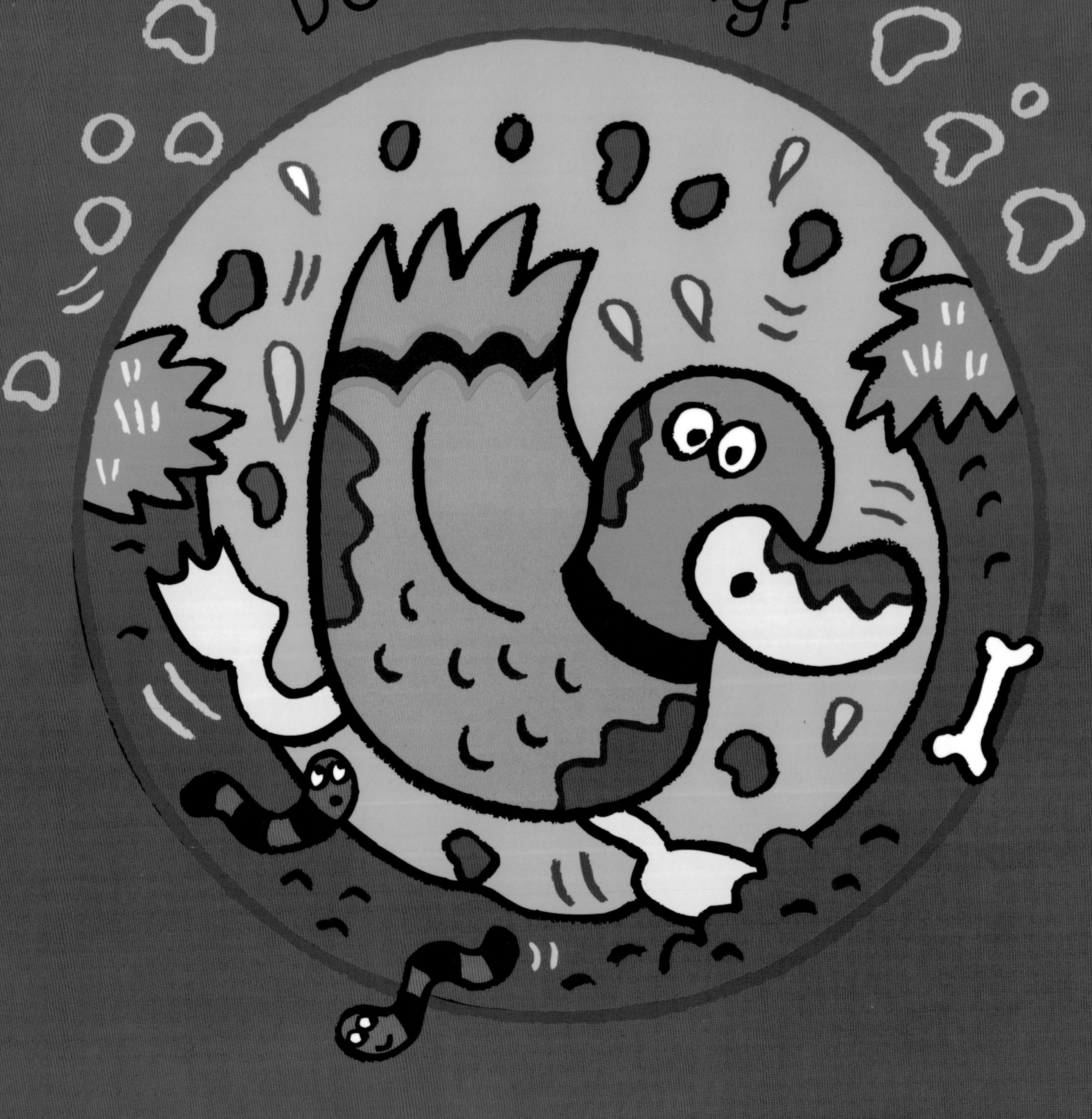

No, but ...

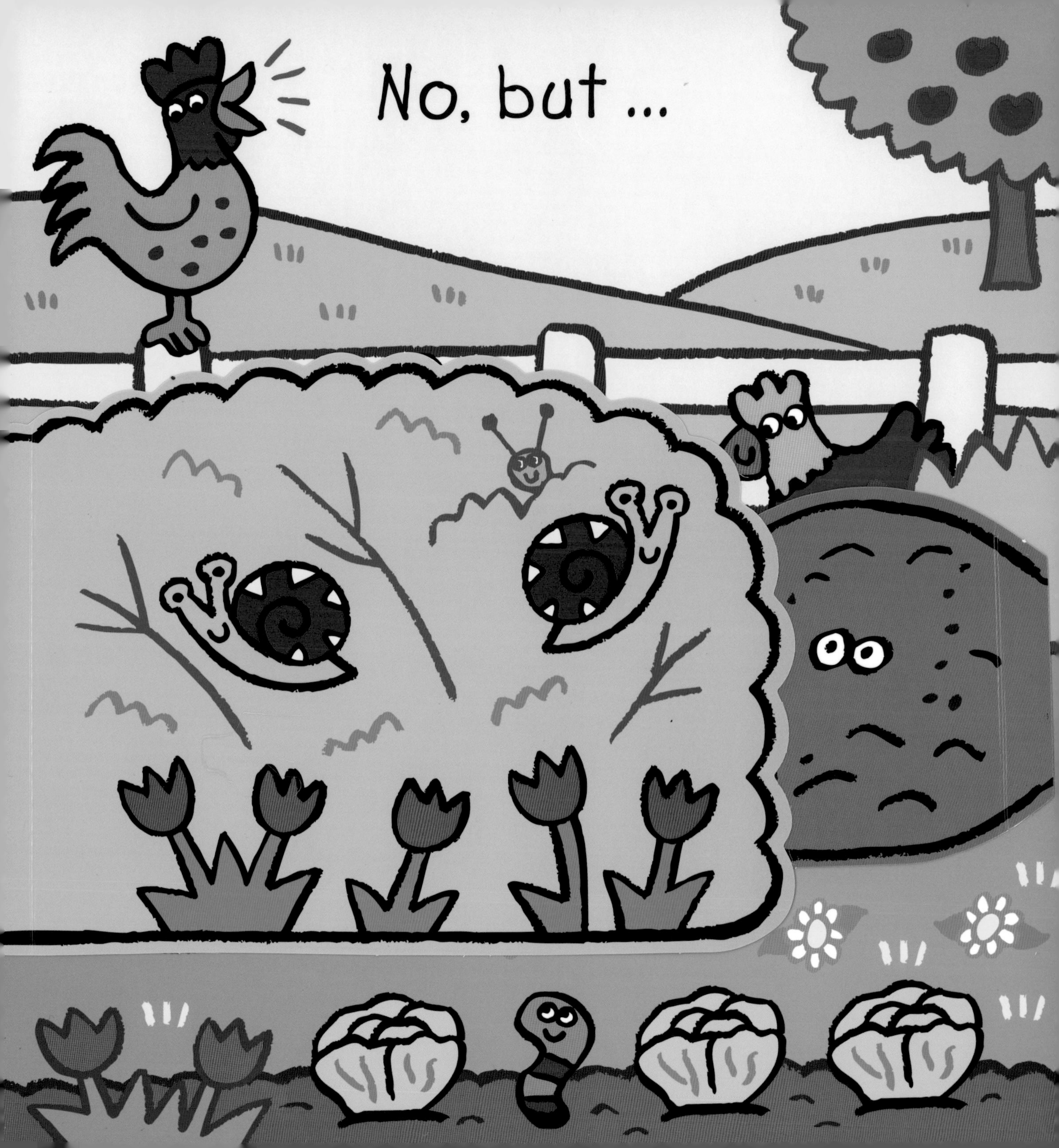

Do jellyfish jump?

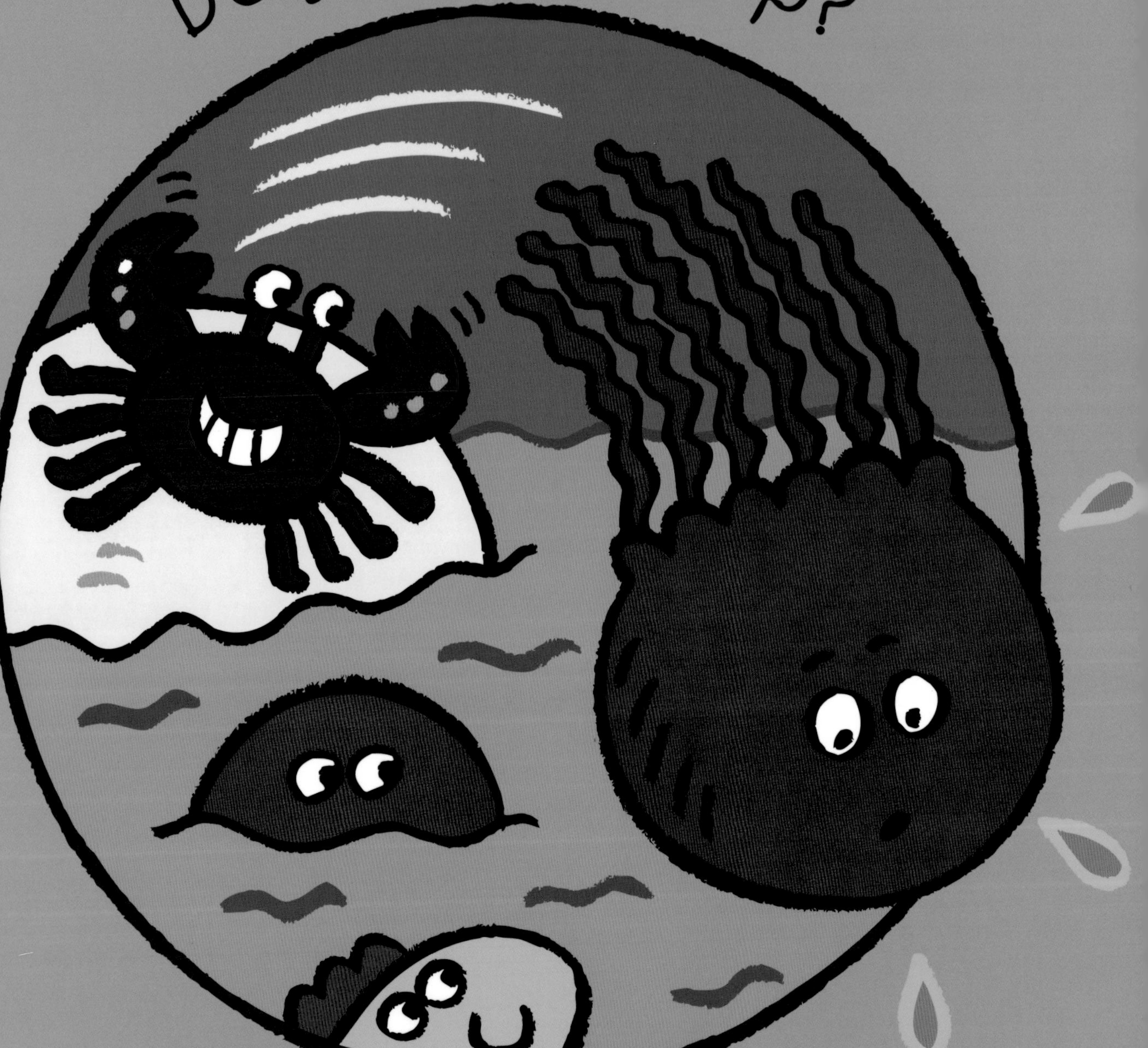

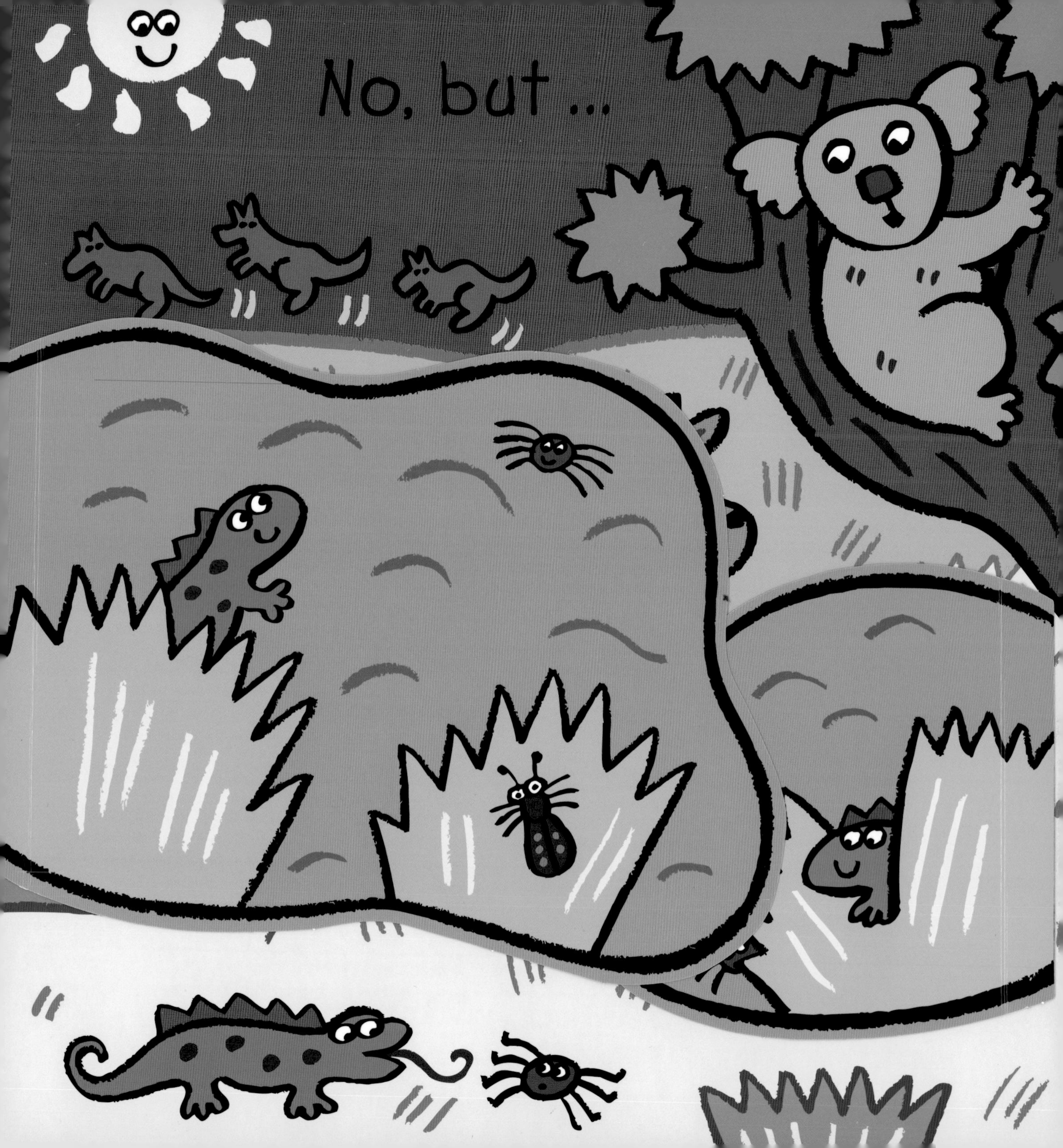
No, but ...

Do spiders slither?

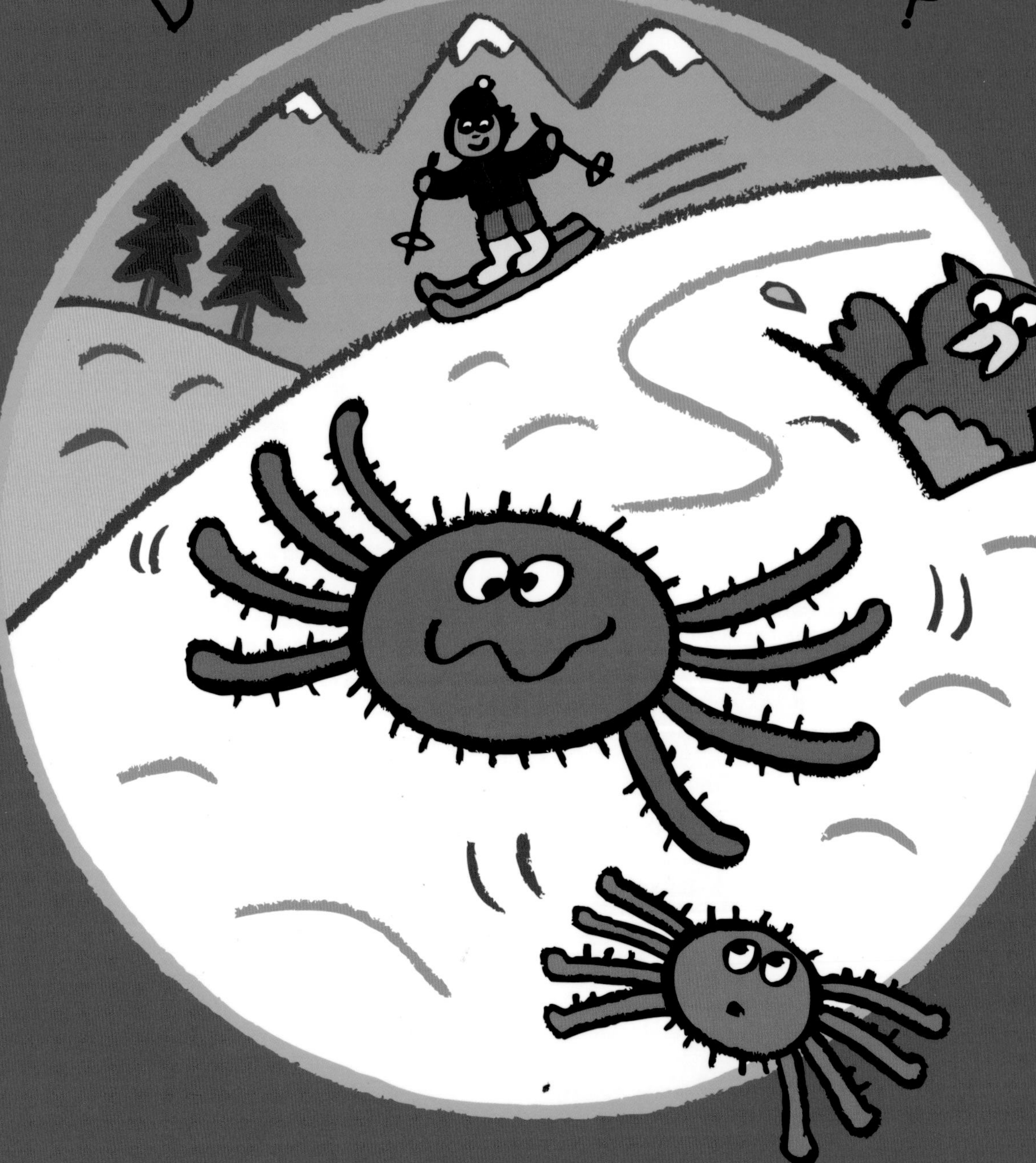

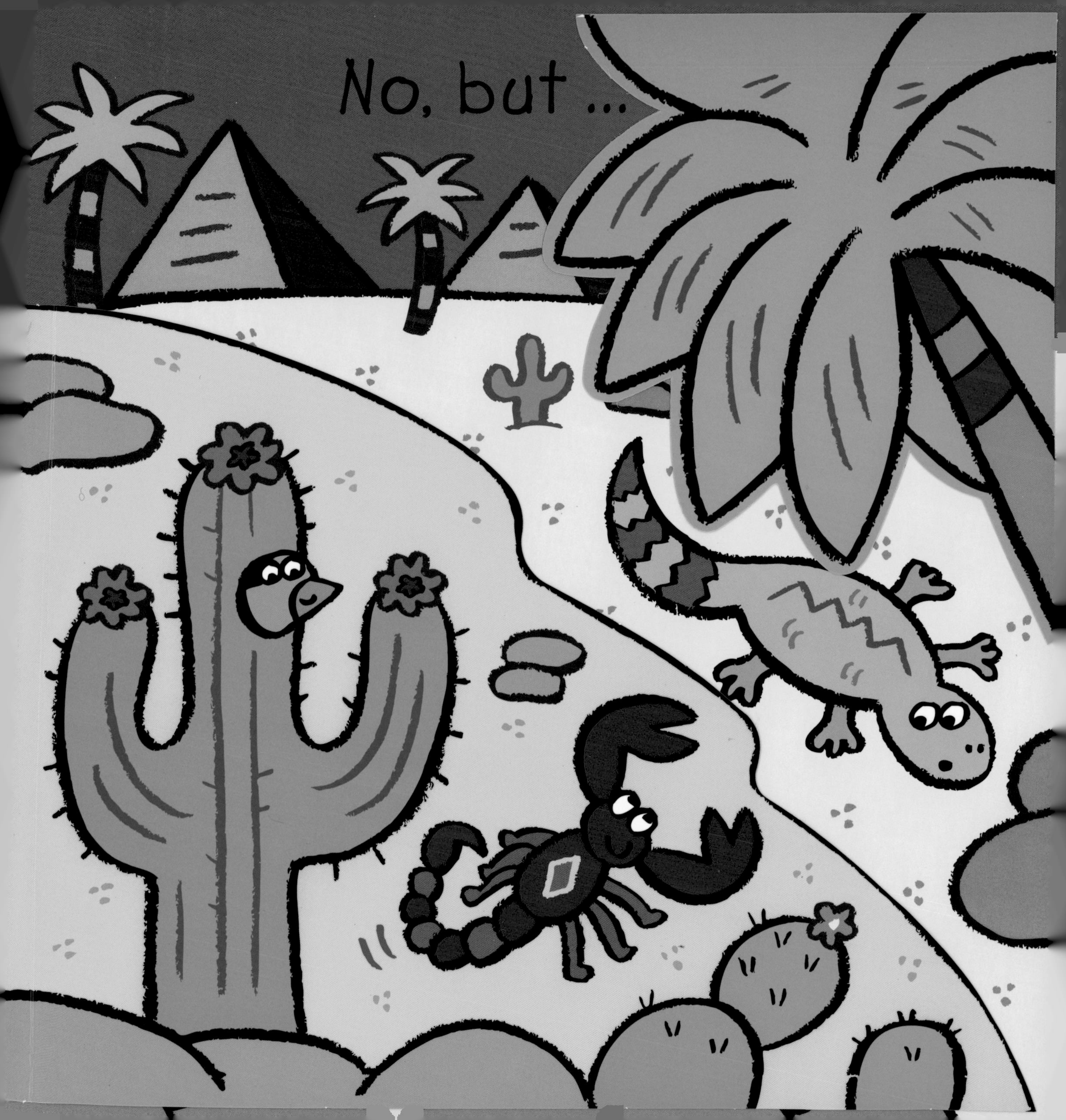
No, but ...

Do frogs fly?

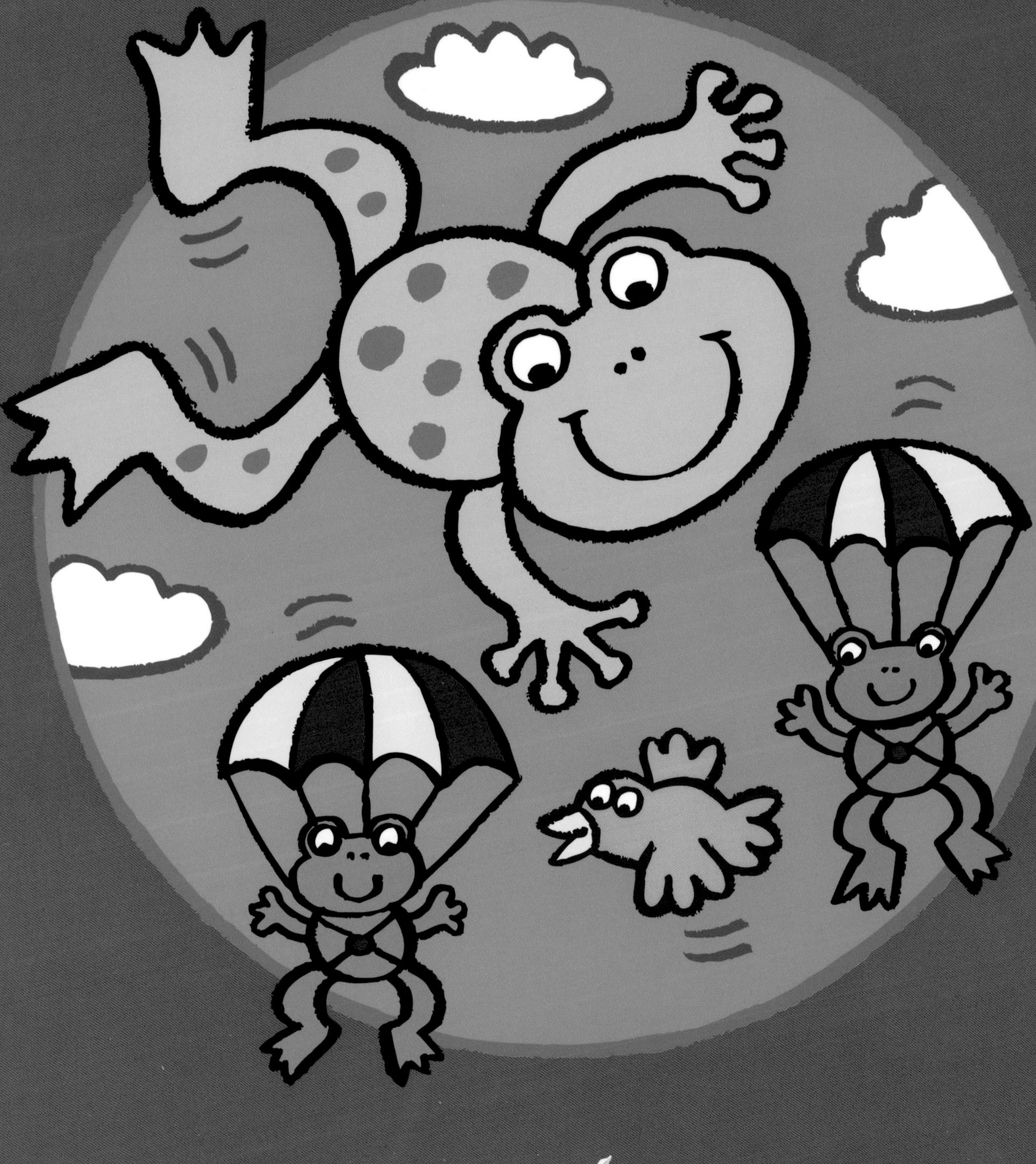

No, but ...

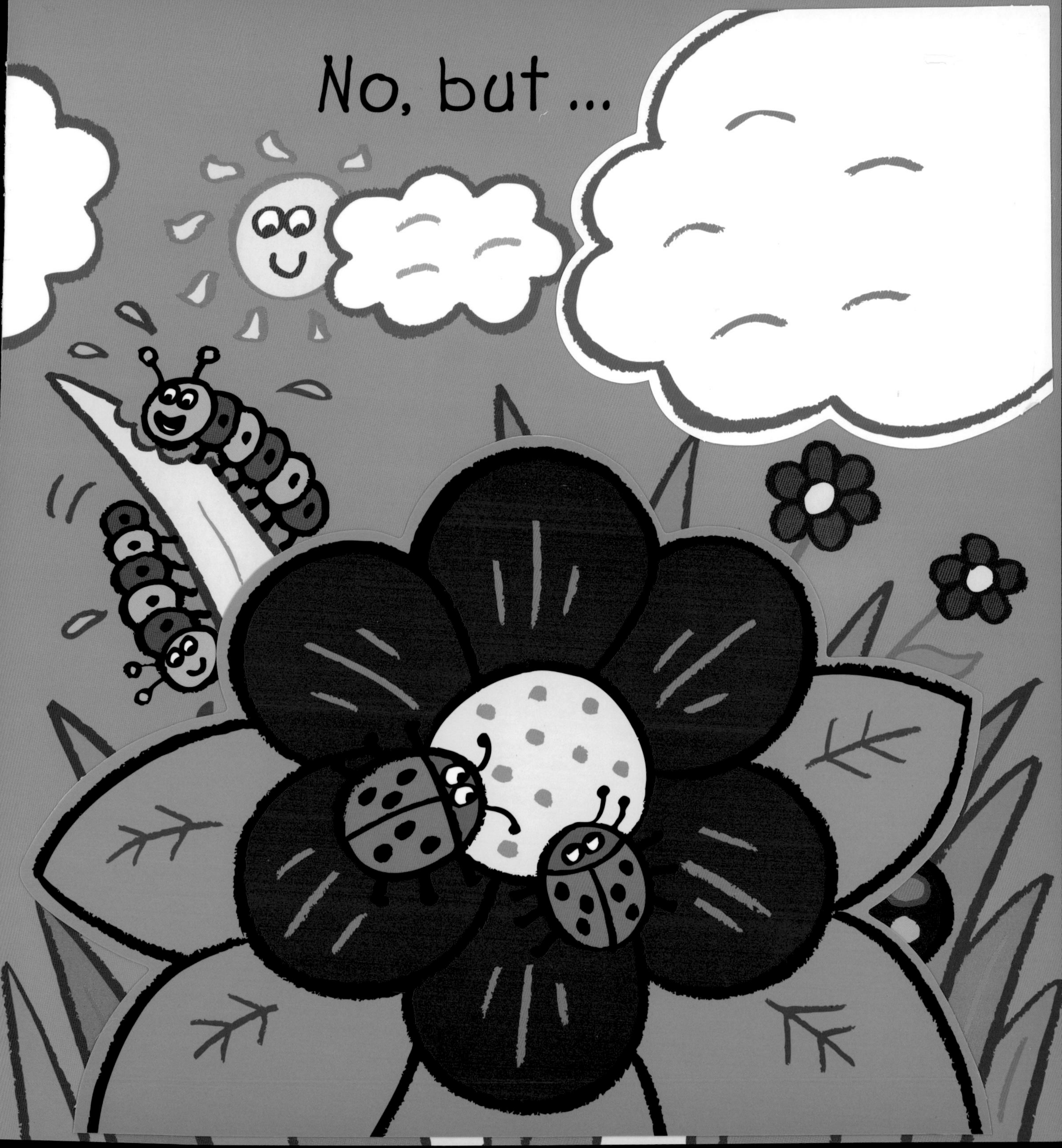

Do guinea pigs gallop?

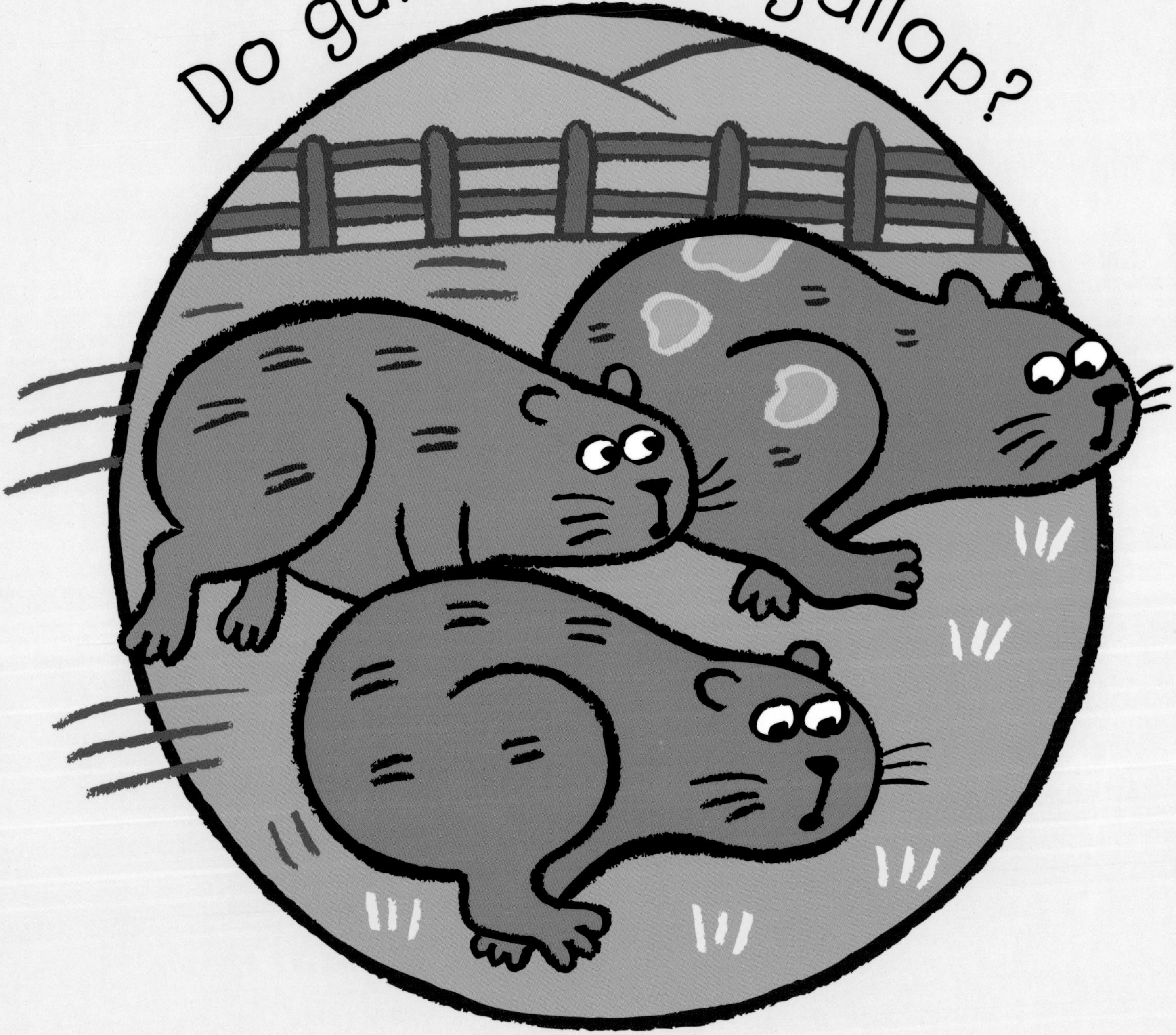

No, but ...

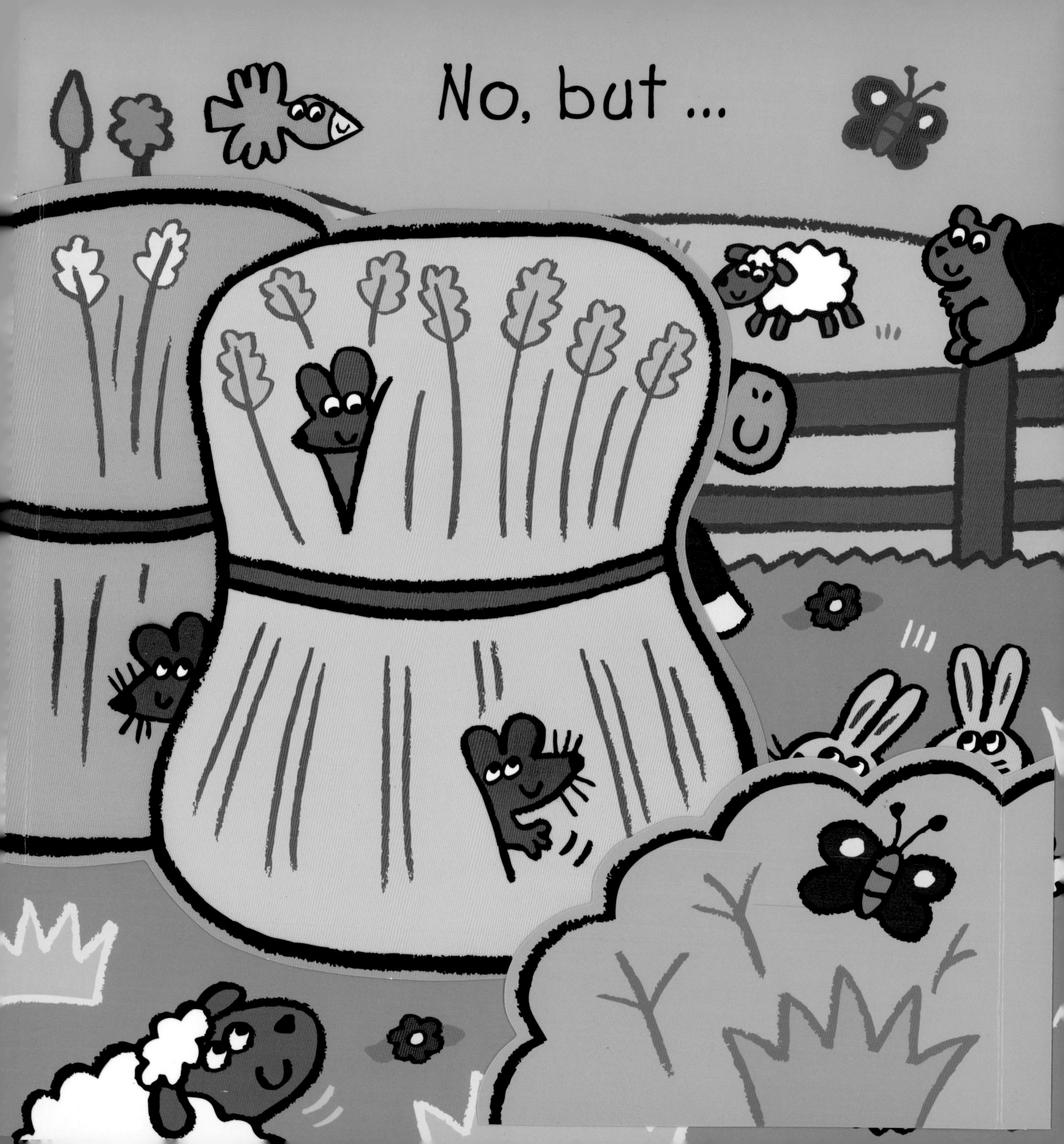

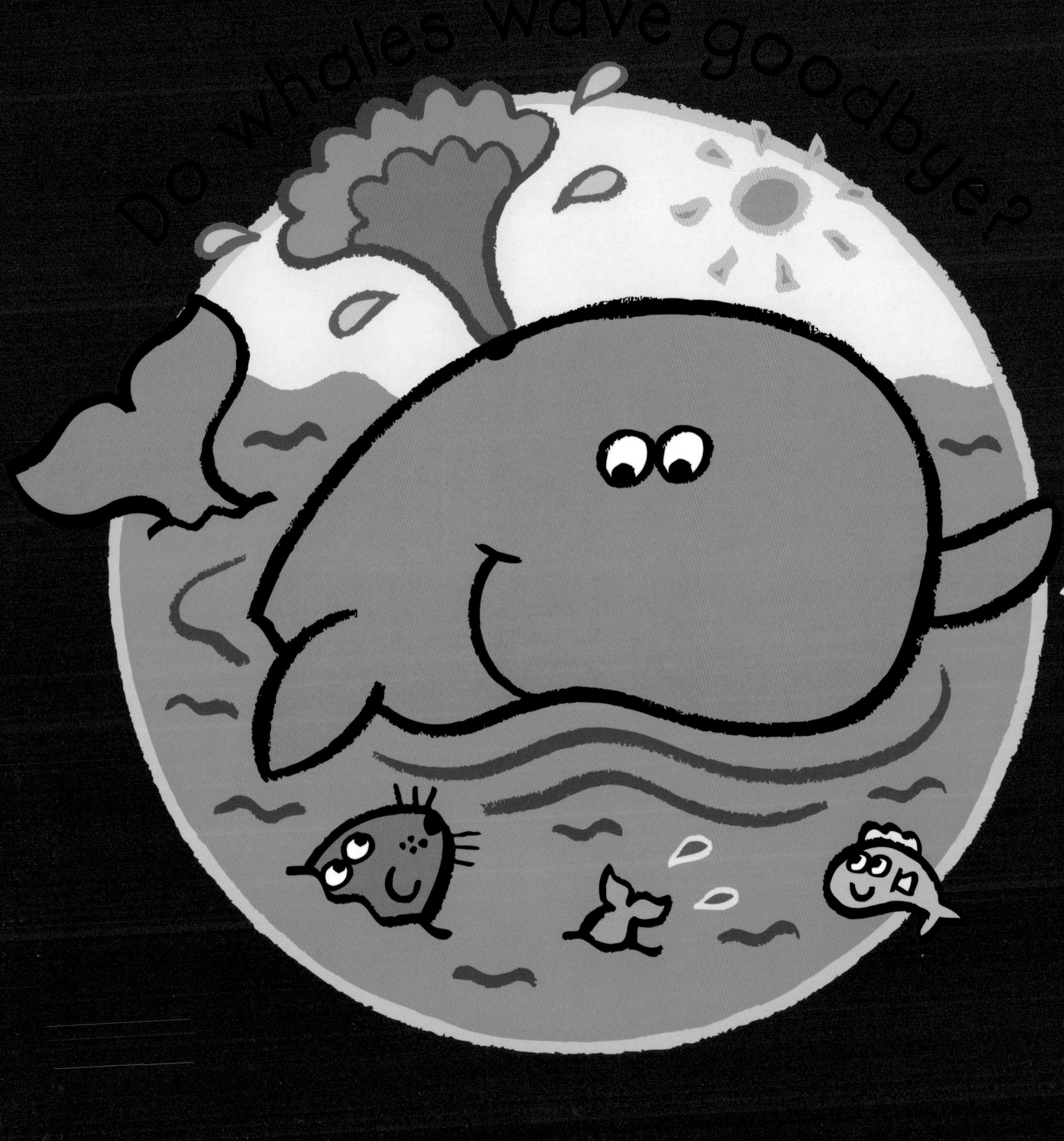
Do whales wave goodbye?

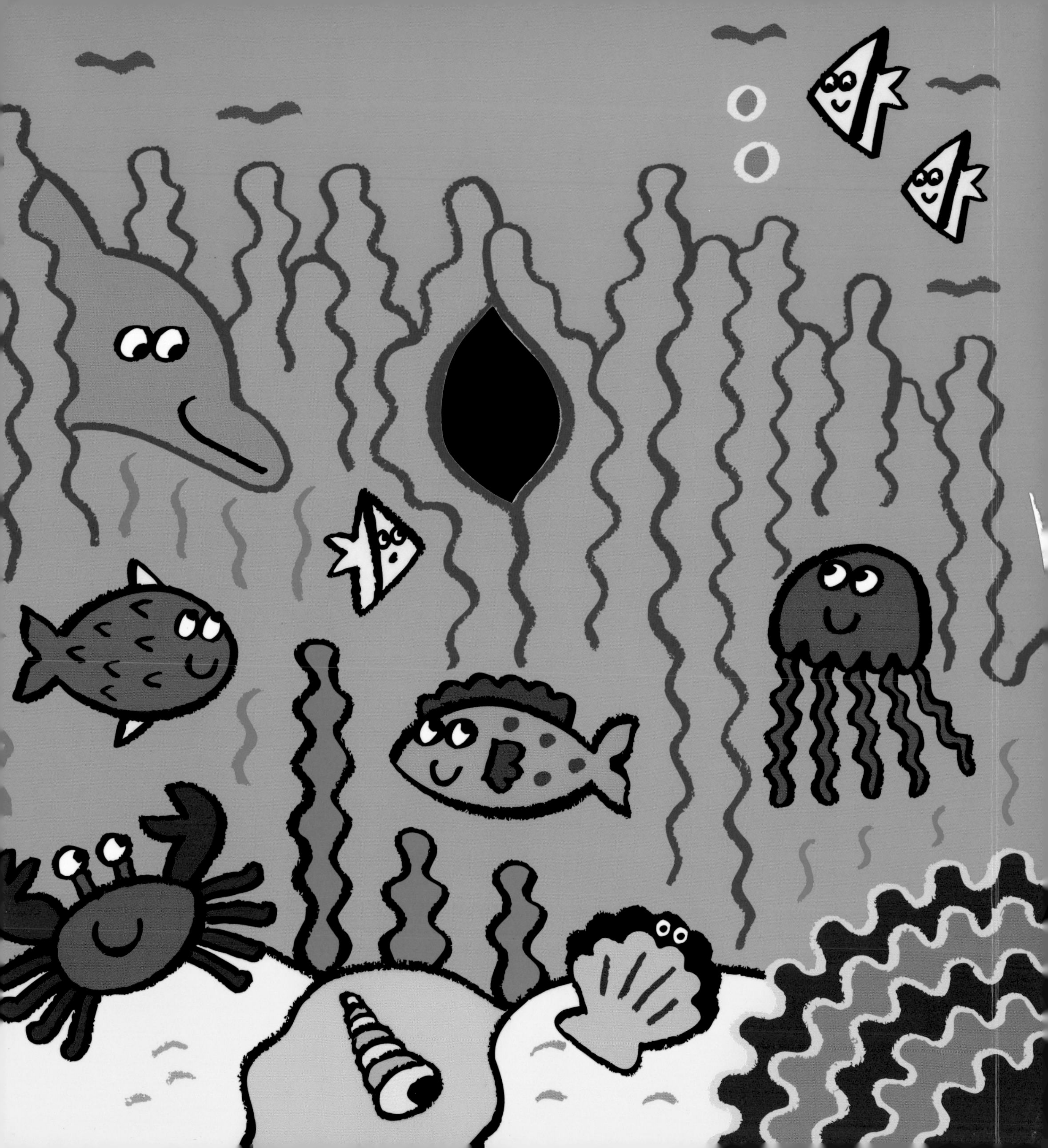

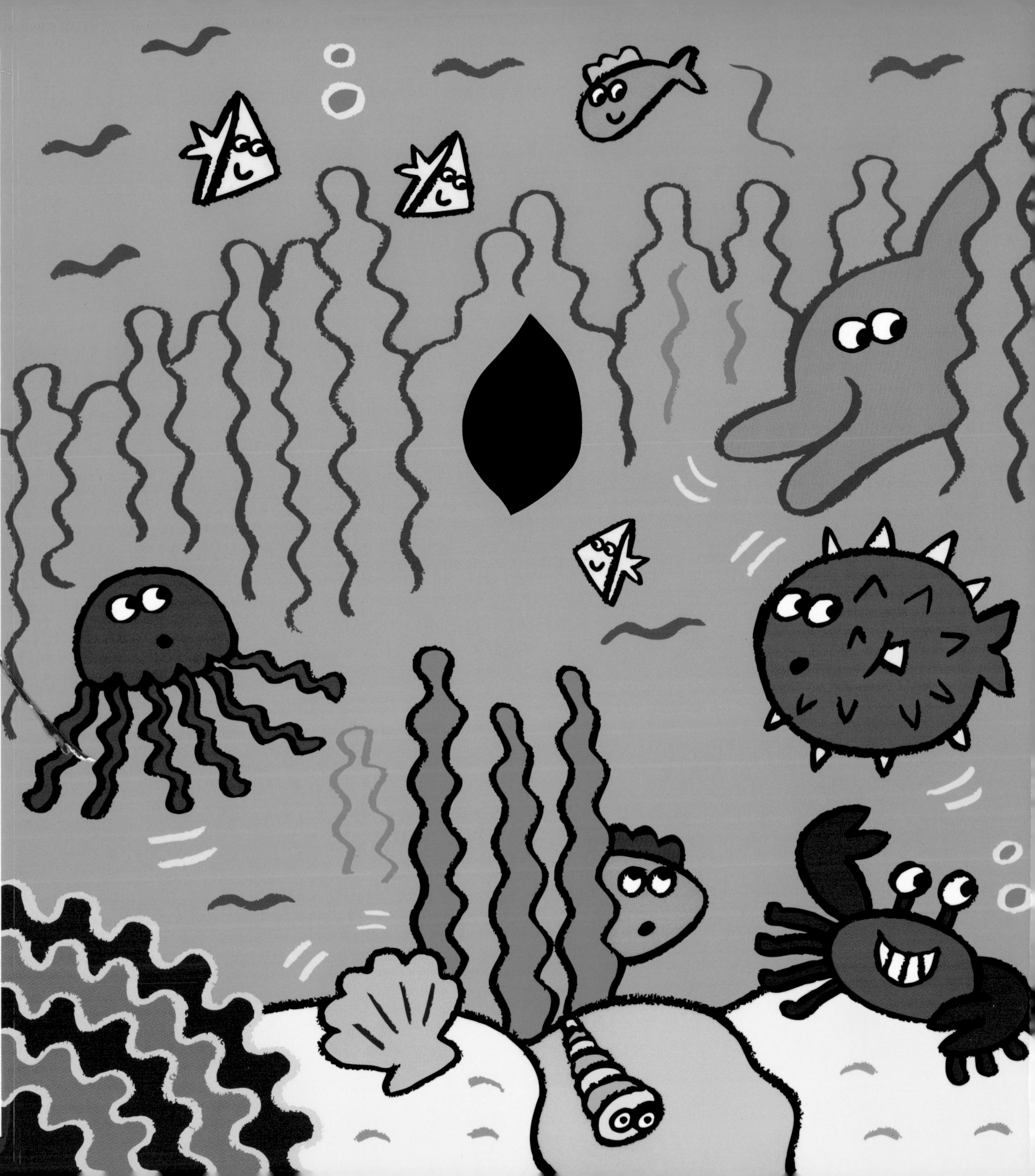